Ladybird  Readers

The Red Knight

Series Editor: Sorrel Pitts
Text adapted by Sorrel Pitts
Illustrated by Emma McCann

LADYBIRD BOOKS

UK | USA | Canada | Ireland | Australia
India | New Zealand | South Africa

Ladybird Books is part of the Penguin Random House group of companies
whose addresses can be found at global.penguinrandomhouse.com.
www.penguin.co.uk   www.puffin.co.uk   www.ladybird.com

Penguin
Random House
UK

First published 2016
001

Copyright © Ladybird Books Ltd, 2016

The moral rights of the author and illustrator have been asserted.

Printed in China

A CIP catalogue record for this book is available from the British Library

ISBN: 978–0–241–25384–7

Ladybird Readers

The Red Knight

Picture words

armor

break

castle

joust

gold coin

knight

lance

In the old days, there was a boy called Tom. His older brother Will was a knight, and Tom wanted to be a knight like him.

One day, Will had to leave.

He gave Tom a gold coin.

"Put this around your neck. Don't lose it," he said. "I have one that's the same."

Tom didn't see Will again, but he often thought about him.

Tom grew older and he started working for an old knight. He helped the knight to clean his armor and his lance.

Then, the old knight died.
Tom was very sad because
he had no one to help.
But he started working
with the horses at the castle.

Tom liked his job with the horses, but he really wanted to be a knight like his brother.

One day, a knight in red
armor came to the castle.
Many people came out of
their houses to see him.

"Who are you?" they asked.

"I am the Red Knight," said the knight. "Who wants to joust with me?"

"I want to joust with you," said a knight. "My boy here can help me with my armor and lance."

"I haven't got a boy," said the Red Knight. "Is there one here who can help me?"

"I can help you," said Tom.
"I was a knight's boy before
and I can be your boy now."

Tom helped the Red Knight
with his lance and his armor.

Many people came to see the joust.
The knights held their lances in
front of them. Their horses were
ready and they ran fast.

Then, the Red Knight's lance broke! Tom ran fast and quickly gave him a new one.

31

The Red Knight won the joust!
"Well done, Red Knight!"
called all the people.

33

"Thank you for helping me,"
said the Red Knight to Tom.
Tom was very happy.

Tom helped the Red Knight
with his horse.

He helped the Red Knight
with his armor.

Then, Tom saw a gold coin
around the Red Knight's neck.

Tom wore the same gold coin
around his neck!

"My brother gave me this gold coin!" said Tom. "Your coin is the same. Are you Will, my older brother?" he asked.

"Yes, Tom. I'm your brother," said the Red Knight.

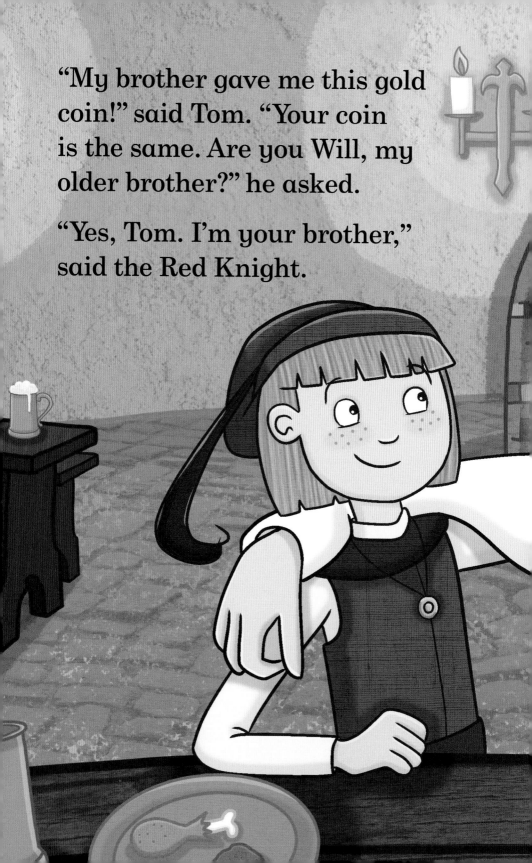

"Do you want to work for me again?" Will asked.

"Yes!" said Tom.

Tom helped his older brother with his armor and lances.

"Soon you can be a knight, like me," Will said. And Tom was very happy!

Activities

The key below describes the skills practiced in each activity.

Spelling and writing

Reading

Speaking

Critical thinking

Preparation for the Cambridge Young Learners Exams

1 **Look and read. Choose the correct words and write them on the lines.**

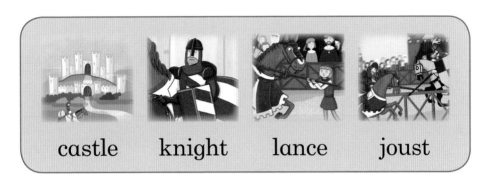

castle   knight   lance   joust

1 In the old days, this was a game between two men on horses. ...... joust ......

2 This is a man who jousted in the past. ....

3 Men used this when they jousted. ....

4 This is the place where knights lived. ....

2 Look and read. Choose the correct words and write them on the lines.

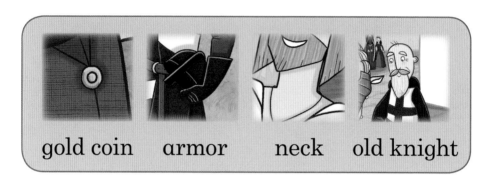

gold coin   armor   neck   old knight

1 One day, Will gave Tom

a _____ gold coin _____ .

2 "Put this around your

_____ ," Will said.

3 Tom started working for

an _____ .

4 He helped the knight to clean

his _____ .

3 Work with a friend.

Talk about the two pictures.

How are they different? 🗨

a

In the old days, there was a boy called Tom. His older brother Will was a knight, and Tom wanted to be a knight like him.

b

One day, Will had to leave.

He gave Tom a gold coin.

"Put this around your neck. Don't lose it," he said. "I have one that's the same."

Tom didn't see Will again but he often thought about him.

Example:

> In picture a,
> Will is not there.

> In picture b,
> Will is there.

4 Look and read.
Write *yes* or *no*.

Then, the old knight died.
Tom was very sad because
he had no one to help.
But he started working
with the horses at the castle.

12   13

1 The old knight died. .... yes ....

2 Tom was very sad. ....

3 There were lots of people ....
to help.

4 Tom started working ....
with horses.

5 The horses were on ....
a farm.

5 **Read the text. Choose the correct words and write them next to 1—5.** 📖 ✏️ ⬡

be came could wanted was

One day, a knight in red armor

1 ___came___ to the castle. He

2 _____ the Red Knight.

He 3 _____ someone who

could joust with him. But the Red

Knight did not have a boy who

4 _____ help him. Tom said,

"I was a knight's boy before and I can

5 _____ your boy now."

51

6 Work with a friend.
Talk about the two pictures.
How are they different? 💬

a

"Who are you?" they asked.

"I am the Red Knight," said the knight. "Who wants to joust with me?"

b

"I want to joust with you," said a knight. "My boy here can help me with my armor and lance."

Example:

In picture a, Tom is next to the knight.

In picture b, Tom is behind the knight.

7 **Circle the correct word.**

1 The knights' horses were ready
and they **run** / **(ran)** fast.

2 Then, the Red Knight's lance
break / **broke**!

3 Tom ran fast and he **give** / **gave**
the Red Knight a new lance.

4 The Red Knight **win** / **won**
the joust!

5 "Well done, Red Knight!"
called / **calls** all the people.

8 **Read the questions.**
Write the answers. 📖 ✏️

1 What did the Red Knight's lance do?

It broke.

2 Who ran and got a new one?

3 Who won the joust?

4 Were the people happy because the Red Knight won?

5 Did the Red Knight speak to Tom after the joust?

9 Look at the pictures. One picture is different. How is it different? Tell your teacher. 💬

Picture d is different because it is not Tom.

10 Choose the best answer.

1 A knight in red armor came to the
   a castle.   **b** house.

2 The people came out of their
   a houses.   **b** castles.

3 They asked him,
   a "Where are you from?"
   b "Who are you?"

4 The Red Knight asked,
   a "Who wants to joust with me?"
   b "Who has got a horse?"

11 **Ask and answer the questions with a friend.** 🗨

"I can help you," said Tom. "I was a knight's boy before and I can be your boy now."

1 How many knights are there?

There are two knights.

2 Where is Tom?

3 What is Tom saying to the Red Knight?

4 What are the Red Knight and his horse wearing?

12 **Read the text. Write some words to complete the sentences about the story.** 📖 ✏️ ⭐

We don't see knights in armor today but in the old days there were lots of them. Knights wore armor and carried lances in a joust. The stronger and quicker knight won the joust.

1 Knights lived in the ⎯old days⎯

in many countries.

2 When they jousted, knights carried

a ⎯⎯⎯⎯⎯⎯⎯⎯⎯ .

3 Knights had to be ⎯⎯⎯⎯⎯⎯

⎯⎯⎯⎯⎯⎯⎯ to win a joust.

13 **Circle the correct picture.**

1 What did the knight's boy have to do when a lance broke?

2 How did the knight's boy help with the armor?

3 Which brother is older?

4 Which knight is leaving the castle?

14 **Read the text and choose the best answer.** 📖 ⭕

1 How did Tom feel when Will left?

（**a** He felt very sad.）

b He felt very happy.

2 Did Tom enjoy working with the horses?

a Yes, he did.

b Yes, he enjoyed.

3 When did Will come back to the castle?

a He came back after many years.

b He came back the next year.

4 Why didn't Tom know Will when he came back?

a Will wore red armor and Tom couldn't see his brother's face.

b Will wore white armor and he didn't talk to Tom.

15 **Talk to your teacher about knights.** 🔘

1 How did knights travel?

Knights traveled on horses.

2 Did knights need a boy?

3 What was the boy's job?

4 Did knights like living in the castle, do you think?

16 **Ask and answer the questions with a friend.**

1 Have you got a brother?

Yes, I have.

2 Why do younger brothers want to be like their older brothers?

3 Do younger brothers always want to be like their older brothers, do you think?

4 Would you like to have lots of brothers? Why? Why not?

5 Are brothers always friends, do you think?

17 **Look and read.**
Write yes or no.

Tom helped his older brother with his armor and lances.

"Soon you can be a knight, like me," Will said. And Tom was very happy!

45

1 Tom is wearing armor. ....no............

2 Tom helped his brother with his armor and his lances. ....

3 Tom rode his horse behind Will. ....

4 Tom's horse wore armor. ....

Level 3

Sharks

978–0–241–25382–3 ☐

The Jungle Book

978–0–241–25383–0 ☐

The Red Knight

978–0–241–25384–7 ☐

The Elves and the Shoemaker

978–0–241–25385–4 ☐

Now you're ready for Level 4!

Notes
CEFR levels are based on guidelines set out in the Council of Europe's European Framework. Cambridge Young Learners English (YLE) Exams give a reliable indication of a child's progression in learning English.